Joey's Ghost Pumpkin

Fern Pascoe Dooley
Illustrated by Jack Woodson

BROADMAN PRESS
Nashville, Tennessee

© Copyright 1982 • Broadman Press
All Rights reserved.
4245-15
ISBN: 0-8054-4515-3
Dewey Decimal Classification: JF
Library of Congress Catalog Card Number: 81-69695
Printed in the United States of America

To
my beloved husband
Hugh Dooley
who went to be with his Lord on
December 5, 1981
and to
Lucy and Loie Pascoe
my wonderful parents,
and to
Deloris and Bill Greene,
Joey's grandparents

J oey was down in the dumps. He was sad and lonely. He was lonely because he no longer had his best friend and pal, Rascal, to play with him. Rascal was no longer there to get excited and bark about everything Joey did. Rascal had been killed by a fast-moving car, and now there was no one to roam the woods with Joey.

Everybody told Joey that he had to perk up. Everybody said he had to forget Rascal and go on to something new. But what?

Joey looked around him. He needed something to do. He needed something to get him excited.

Joey liked to read, but he had already read all his library books. They were piled by the front door as a big hint to his mother that he desperately needed to go get some new ones. There wasn't a thing in his house to read except that dumb, old seed catalog that had just come in the mail.

Joey began to turn the pages in the catalog: rose bushes, lemon trees, raspberry bushes, avocado trees. Joey liked to read about the things he had seen growing in California when he visited there, but he knew he couldn't plant those things on a Kansas farm. Squash, eggplant, okra, zucchini. He liked the sounds of all those words rolling off his tongue, but everybody in Kansas grew those vegetables. If Joey were going to grow something, he wanted it to be different—totally different.

He turned more pages: corn, tomatoes, watermelons, pumpkins. *Pumpkins!* That word touched Joey's lonely, sad heart. Pumpkins were connected with Halloween, and Halloween was Joey's favorite time of the year. He loved dressing up as Robin Hood or Spider Man or a monster. He loved carving the jack-o'-lantern. He wished his family could afford one of the giant pumpkins he saw on the lot when they went to buy. But they usually came away with a middle-sized one. He guessed he would always have to settle for middle size unless. . . . Suddenly a marvelous idea came to Joey. It was such a grand idea that he felt good all over. He would grow pumpkins, and he could choose the biggest one for his very own.

He read everything underneath the pumpkin seed listings. There was one thing nice about pumpkin seed. They didn't cost very much. If he could get his dad to advance him two weeks' allowance, he could order the seed that night and have them ready to plant on schedule.

Joey could hardly wait for his dad to get home. His dad would be tired, and he knew he must not rush him. Joey's dad was slow and easy-going. But if he were rushed, he would just say no, and that would be the end of that. Joey would have to plan some strategy.

What should he do first? He went out into the garden to see if there were space for a pumpkin patch. There wasn't. But there was lots of space beyond the barn if his dad would agree that he could use it.

Joey was an energetic boy, but he knew he would need some grown-up help to get his pumpkin business going. He was secretly counting on his dad for help.

He walked back into the house and looked around. His room was an untidy mess. His clothes were all over the room. His toys and his books were scattered everywhere. He knew how disappointed his father would be if he came home and found the room in that condition.

Joey walked through the house and picked up everything that was his. There was a lot of it. His arms were piled high. He would have to make a second trip. He was embarrassed. No wonder his dad was always on him about his cluttering. His room looked like a cyclone had struck the middle of it.

After a few minutes of real hard straightening and tidying, Joey stood in his doorway. He looked at his neat room and smiled. He knew that room would pass inspection.

Now what could he do to make his mother happy? She, too, would be tired when she got home from work. He went to the kitchen. He groaned! His mother hated the kitchen. She said it was always full of dirty dishes, and Joey knew that was the truth. He decided to see what he could do about it.

First, he stacked the dishes, put the garbage in the trash can and emptied it. That wasn't difficult. Joey wondered why he always fussed and fumed so much about taking out the garbage.

Back in the kitchen, Joey decided to soak the dishes in a pan of warm sudsy water. He had seen his mother do that. He cleared the table and decided to surprise his mom by setting the table for dinner without being asked.

Joey felt good. He was pleased with himself because he was trying to make other people happy.

Joey didn't like to wash dishes, but today he was in the mood to do even that. He would have to hurry. His folks would be home soon.

At last all the dishes were in the drainer. He had rinsed them carefully. Wouldn't his mom be happy! He gazed around. Everything looked perfect. He went into the living room and turned on the TV. That would help pass the time until his parents got home.

Joey heard the brakes on the car as the car screeched to a halt outside the kitchen. He decided not to move. He would just listen for his parents' reaction. He was so excited that he felt a cold sweat breaking out on his forehead.

Joey could hear the rustling of the grocery sacks being carried into the kitchen. He wanted to get up and help with the groceries, but he didn't. He just listened all the more carefully. Surely his mom and dad would notice what he had done! But they only talked about the brakes. His dad said, "I'm afraid they're unsafe. The screeching doesn't bother me, but safety does. I know we can't afford to have them fixed, but we must. I'll take the car to a mechanic tomorrow."

Joey felt his heart go thud! How could he ask for an advance on his allowance if Dad were already having money problems. Joey decided to wait until after dinner to ask about having a pumpkin patch.

He turned back to the TV. He couldn't believe that neither of his parents noticed all the extra work he had done. Their money problems must be awfully serious.

7

Finally Joey's mother called that dinner was ready. They were having spaghetti. Spaghetti was one of Joey's favorite meals, and his mother had piled his plate high.

"Yummy!" Joey said as he sat down. He hoped he could liven things up a little by getting some conversation going. But his parents just politely passed him food and talked to each other about the car.

"Maybe it's time to get a new car," his father sighed. "Seems like we're pouring money down a rat hole. One problem one month and another one the next."

Mom mumbled, "I agree, but I sure hate to have to start making monthly payments again."

After dinner, Dad suggested, "Let's all go to town and look at cars."

Still not a word about his clean room, the clean house, the table set for dinner, or the empty garbage can. Joey really felt low. He felt worse than he did when he struck out at bat that afternoon at school.

The three of them piled into the pickup truck. Soon they were going from one car lot to another. Joey looked at all the classy cars while his parents looked at the ordinary cars. He cooperated with everything his parents suggested. He wanted to get home where he just might get a chance to talk about pumpkins.

At last his parents decided which car they liked best out of the many they had examined. Joey couldn't see anything super about the car. But he liked the "new" smell of it, and the color was his favorite—bright red. The salesman gave his dad the keys, and his mother drove the car around town. Joey knew they would buy it because both of his parents were smiling and said they would be saving money on gasoline. He just hoped there would be enough money left for pumpkin seed too.

Back at home, Joey's mother said: "It's way past your bedtime, Joey. Get into the tub and then go right to bed, or you'll never get up tomorrow in time for school." She didn't ask about homework. When he had cleaned his room, Joey had laid it all out so that she would see it first thing. But he knew that he'd have to wait until the next day for pumpkin talk.

In the bathtub, he finally let the tears flow freely. He didn't sob. No one must know how hurt he was. Nobody came into his room to tuck him in or to listen to his prayers. He could never remember that happening before. Their money problems must be real big.

He could hear his parents discussing credit union, interest rates, down payments, and the length of time they would be "saddled" with monthly payments. He pulled the covers over his head, closed his eyes, and prayed, "Heavenly Father, please help me to get some pumpkin seed."

At school the next day, the teacher seemed very pleased when the county 4-H Club adviser stopped by for a visit. He gave some pamphlets to the students suggesting things for them to do during the coming summer months. Joey wasn't very interested until he heard Mr. Billings say: "I do hope some of you will plant pumpkins for the county fair contest. Last year no one won the twenty-five-dollar prize because nobody entered! And that beautiful set of encyclopedias is still in my office because no one did a research paper on squash, melons, or pumpkins."

There was that word again—*pumpkins*! Joey felt he must have pumpkins on the brain. Right now his mouth was watering for a piece of pumpkin pie. He was going to ask his mother to bake him one.

Joey stuffed the contest leaflets into his knapsack. That was what he needed to get his conversation going tonight. He had listened carefully as Mr. Billings explained how to grow pumpkins. It would really be very simple— just a lot of hard digging.

After he got off the bus, Joey walked home slowly. There was no use to hurry. There was no Rascal to play with, and his mother wouldn't be home for an hour or so.

He let himself into the house and looked around him. It was just like yesterday. The sink was piled high with dishes; the trash was overflowing, his bed wasn't made—

9

the family had just gotten up too late to do anything.

Suddenly he was upset. He had tried so hard the night before, and no one had noticed a thing. Should he try again? He hated to wash spaghetti dishes, but he knew he should. He filled the sink with sudsy water and turned the sound on the TV up high enough to be heard in the kitchen. It wasn't as good as watching and listening, but this way he could get things cleaned up before his parents got home.

Cleaning his room was easy. Maybe if he would just put things away every day, he wouldn't have so many hassles over the way his room looked. There were no piles of clothing. He had hung them all up the night before. So very shortly, he was back in the kitchen.

He unloaded the dish drainer before he began. Everything in the sink was easy until he got to the spaghetti pan. He could hear his mother complaining about washing up after a spaghetti meal. He agreed with everything she had ever said—but spaghetti was still his favorite food!

Tonight he was going to set the table with different dishes, and he was going to use those new yellow place mats that he had given his mother for her birthday. They would catch her eye. She'd surely notice.

Next he folded all the paper sacks from last night's groceries. They got lots of paper sacks every time they went to town. He looked at the nice, neat stack of sacks. He should put them away, but he didn't. He wanted his mother to see that he had folded them the way she had taught him just a week ago, but he did empty the trash. He got all the trash out of the bathroom. He decided to hang up all the towels that were all over the floor. He counted five towels, and there were only three people in his family. His mother must have washed her hair last night because she always used three towels for that.

When everything was in order, he took a tour of the house. He folded yesterday's newspapers into a neat stack. He put the seed catalog right on top. Tonight he would get around to talking about pumpkins.

Joey took out his homework. He must have it all done by dinner time. He wasn't going to let any little or big problems get in his way.

He heard those screechy brakes grind as the car came to a halt, and soon his mother hurried through the door. She called out to him as she passed through the house, "Joey, we're going into town to meet Daddy and pick up the new car. We'll get something to eat while we wait for all the paperwork to be done. I will be ready to go as soon as I locate the title to the old car. By the way, you should look in the trunk of the car to be sure nothing is left in it. Your dad said he thought your baseball gear might be in there." She didn't see a thing he had done.

Joey moseyed out to the car. His spirits were so low that he was near tears. It didn't seem to matter what he did. He just couldn't get his parents' attention. Perhaps when Old Screechy Brakes was gone, the family could get around to talking again.

When they got to the restaurant, Joey ordered the cheapest dinner on the menu. He was doing his best to help with the family money problem. But he noticed that his parents seemed to order just as usual. He didn't understand adults! They talked about high interest, carrying charges, monthly payments, and then ordered big desserts. They said that they were celebrating the new car. They didn't even notice how he had ordered the cheapest dinner he could!

The new car had been washed and waxed, and it smelled new. The motor just hummed as they drove through the countryside. His parents were talking about taking a vacation now that they had the new car.

He tried to break into the conversation. He said, "The county 4-H advisor came to school yesterday. He wants all of us to get started on our spring and summer projects. He said planning ahead was the very best way. I've got a real good idea, but I need your help!"

"Not tonight, Joey," said his mother. "This is a very

special night for your dad and me. We have just bought our very first new car. We want to relax and celebrate. No planning projects tonight!''

Joey hoped he could get out of the car and into his room before he began crying. He just might not cry if no one talked to him. But that big, hard lump in his throat had been there for two days. He went immediately to the bathroom and started the water running into the tub. That would cover up any sounds his sniffles made.

His parents stayed outside and walked around the car, admiring it. They were really pleased. He wished he could get as excited as they were, but Old Screechy Brakes had never bothered him. He and Rascal had loved the backseat of that old car.

Joey couldn't face his parents just then. He didn't want them to be unhappy. He just wanted to be happy too.

They were still talking about the expense of a vacation when they came into the house. Joey could hear his dad explaining they would have to save more money than they ever had before. His mother said that she'd be willing to do it if he and Joey would.

Joey had never felt selfish before, but at that moment he felt very selfish. He wanted pumpkin seed more than he wanted a family vacation. He needed something to do after school every day. It was very lonely living two miles away from the closest neighbor.

Joey had gone to his room without taking his bath. He took out all the pamphlets he had gotten from the 4-H advisor and began to read them again. Suddenly his eye caught something he hadn't seen before. How could he have missed that? It was all the information he would need to enter the annual Halloween Pumpkin Contest sponsored by the chamber of commerce. He wondered what the chamber of commerce was, but he knew one thing for sure—they always gave away lots of prizes. Joey liked to work for prizes. Even if he didn't win, he enjoyed dreaming that he would someday.

There were to be three prizes. Naturally there would

always be a prize for the biggest pumpkin. That was a savings bond. Joey had two twenty-five-dollar bonds, but this one was a fifty-dollar bond. He was going to try hard for that.

The next prize was for the ugliest jack-o'-lantern. Joey was artistic. Everybody said so, especially his grandma. She encouraged him to enter every art contest, and he had won three first prizes. He'd really work on ideas for that contest.

This year there was a new prize—for the most unusual pumpkin. What would cause a pumpkin to be unusual? All the pumpkins he had ever seen were very much alike, except for size. He would check out the seed catalog. It just might give him some ideas.

He jumped out of bed and started to get the catalog, but his dad stopped him with: "Get into bed right this minute! It's thirty minutes past your bedtime."

Joey didn't think he could handle any more disappointments. No one had noticed that he hadn't taken his bath. He surely wasn't going to mention it. He turned off his light and was soon asleep.

It was Friday. Joey always liked Fridays because of the afternoon baseball games. He hoped the teacher would select him to choose a team. She always said that Joey chose well, that he selected the best players not just his best friends.

At three o'clock, everyone went outside the building to get the game started. Sure enough, Mrs. Kellogg asked Joey to choose a team. His best friend, Bart, would choose against him. Luck was with him when they flipped a coin for first choice. He chose Roberto. With him as pitcher, Joey knew his team would win even before the first ball was thrown.

It was a good game, and everybody played well on both sides. When the school bus drove up, the game had to stop. The noisy group clambered onto the bus. Mrs. Kellogg waved good-bye as the bus lumbered down the highway.

Joey was the last person to get off the bus. From habit, he looked for Rascal. That lump came back in his throat when he remembered that Rascal wouldn't ever be there to meet him again. He walked slowly down the road to his house, stopping on the way to get the mail.

There was a letter from his grandma in California. He opened it quickly because it was addressed to Joey McClintock, and that was his name. He could not believe it when he found a crazy April Fool card, and out of it fell three one-dollar bills.

"Oh, you sweet, wonderful Grandma," Joey shouted to himself. "Maybe our money problems aren't so bad. Maybe this will buy all the pumpkin seed I need."

Joey ran into the house and headed straight for the seed catalog. He knew that prices had all gone up since he ordered carrot and radish seed last year, but he didn't have any idea how much.

He turned to the pumpkin pages. He was so excited that his breath came in gasps. That's what his mother didn't like. She always said, "Joey, you get too emotional about everything." He guessed he'd have to admit that he did get carried away with about every idea that popped into his head.

Pumpkin seed were really high-priced. The big, big pumpkins were what he looked for first. He really wanted a chance at that fifty-dollar bond. If he read the captions correctly, he could get seventy-five super-duper grand, deluxe seeds for a dollar. "Money just doesn't go very far when you're spending it," he thought sadly.

He looked at every pictured pumpkin. He was just about to close the catalog when an ad for albino pumpkin seeds caught his eye. Joey knew what the word *albino* meant, but he was puzzled about that ad. Were the seed white? Was the inside of the pumpkin white? Or was the outside of the pumpkin white? What a joke that would be! A pumpkin patch filled with ghost pumpkins!

15

Excitement gripped Joey. He couldn't believe it. If albino pumpkins were white on the outside, Joey McClintock was going to win that unusual pumpkin contest. If only he could get his parents settled down to talking to him long enough to order his seed.

He folded and unfolded his three dollars. He must write to his grandma. It was too bad that she lived so very far away. She was the one person who was always willing to listen to anything Joey had to say. They could talk for hours, and she never told him that his ideas weren't good ones.

Joey was in no mood to do his chores, but he knew he couldn't overlook them; so he got up and got busy. There was only a little trash. Only cereal bowls were left on the kitchen table. Dishes were not his job, and nobody had noticed when he had done them the last few days. Still he had found a good deal of pleasure in trying to be helpful. He knew deep down that his mother liked it when he showed that he was responsible.

He quickly made his bed, hung up a few clothes, and put all the dirty clothes from his hamper into the laundry room. He was proud of himself. That was the first time he had ever done that without being asked to do it.

Towels were scattered over the bathroom floor again. Five of them. His mother had beautiful hair, and she washed it often. He wondered if washing made it beautiful. If that were true, pretty hair caused messy bathrooms. He couldn't put all those towels into the clothes hamper; so he just unloaded the hamper into the laundry room too. That made two good things he had done today without being asked. Now that he didn't have Rascal to romp with and feed, he seemed to have a lot of time on his hands. Besides, the days were getting longer.

Joey turned on the TV. He had hardly watched it all week. Sometimes he got tired of TV. He would much rather work at a project with somebody. He liked it when his dad had a job to do on Saturdays because he usually let him go along.

17

The new car quietly entered the driveway. Right behind it came his dad's pickup. Good. They were both home early! But Joey's mother seemed in a rush.

"Joey" she said, "go out into the garage and see if your dad has any walnuts he can pick out for me quickly. I need a cupful of nuts for that good orange peel cake I'm going to take to the church supper tonight. Tell him we need to get into high gear immediately."

Joey ran quickly. If they had to go somewhere, Joey was glad it was to a potluck supper. Joey McClintock and potluck meals went hand in hand. He didn't remember ever missing one.

He knew he'd have to get all cleaned up; so he decided to get it over with. He would have a good time at church. All his friends would be there. They would eat and play while the grown-ups talked about building a new church.

Joey knew they must need a new building or the adults wouldn't be talking about it so much, but he didn't see why. Their roof didn't leak. The building did have creaky floors, but those floors didn't bother anyone except the adults. He and his friends enjoyed hearing the old floors squeak when the church ushers brought visitors down the aisles on Sunday mornings. Those squeaks just gave him and his friends something to giggle about.

Joey's mom was surprised when she saw his clean clothes and combed hair. "I should have known that you'd be ready for a potluck meal," she laughed. "Here, take this cake out to the car, and put it carefully on the backseat floor. I'm going to get a half-gallon of my good pickled peaches because everybody likes them so much."

Kansas farmers were generous people. Their potluck meals were like Thanksgiving dinners regardless of the time of year.

The McClintocks were a little late. They always were, but that was because Joey's mother worked and they lived farther away than any of the other people. Joey's mother always brought desserts. She could get her food on the big dessert table before people got to that part of the meal.

18

Everybody was glad to see them. Joey knew other people liked his mom and dad. They were always greeted so warmly. Tonight everyone was talking about the McClintock's new car. He decided that cars must be about the most important thing in the world to adults. Even some of the kids acted like getting a new car was mighty special.

Finally all the eating, talking, and playing began to slow down. Farmers go to bed early because they must get up early. All the ladies gathered up their empty dishes, and the families began to pile into their cars. Neighbors came over to admire the McClintock's new car as they passed by. Joey's parents beamed. Their new car was really a great joy to them.

Early Saturday morning, Joey was awakened by his father tousling his hair.

"Get up, big boy," he said. "Your Uncle Dennis and I are going fishing. We thought you might enjoy going along."

Fishing was one of Joey's favorite things. But today he didn't want to go fishing. He just wanted a chance to talk to his father about pumpkins, pumpkin seed, and a 4-H project. However, he couldn't talk to his dad if he were off fishing. Besides, Uncle Dennis might know something about pumpkins.

Joey dressed hurriedly. His mother was seated at the breakfast table, talking to his uncle and his father when Joey entered the kitchen. She quickly cooked a plate of buttermilk pancakes for Joey and talked about how much she enjoyed going fishing when she was a girl. Joey finished his pancakes quickly. He and his dad put their fishing gear in Uncle Dennis's pickup.

They traveled a long, long way, at least it seemed long to Joey. Mr. McClintock and Uncle Dennis worked together every day. Joey was always amazed that they always talked about work when they were together. Joey wiggled and squirmed in his seat between the two men. He just couldn't think of a way to break into the conversation. If he just said, "I want us to talk about pumpkins," he wondered what the men would do. Instead, he sidestepped the issue a little and asked, "Can either of you tell me what an albino pumpkin is?"

"Sure can't," said Uncle Dennis. "Never heard of such. I think you may be mixed up. I've heard of albino horses, pigs, and cows, but I never heard of albino pumpkins. A ghost pumpkin—that's what it would be."

"Son, you'd better talk to the county agent," his father advised. "He's the one who knows all about plants."

That ended the talk about pumpkins for the moment, as they had finally reached the lake.

They fished for a long time. After two hours with no bites, the wind began to come up. It sloshed the waves against the boat.

"Better get off the lake," yelled Joey's dad. "We aren't really safe when the waves are this high."

Returning home seemed shorter than going. It always did to Joey. Down deep he was happy. Maybe he'd get to talk to his parents after he got home.

When they got out of the truck, Joey heard his father say, "Dennis, I'm putting a five dollar bill here to help pay for the gasoline we used."

Joey was already out of the truck and was waving his arms wildly in his joy to be home. He liked his uncle Dennis, but he hoped he wouldn't stay long. He wanted his parents all to himself for awhile. He felt that he just couldn't wait any longer than tonight for his pumpkin talk.

Joey was almost hilarious with joy. He could see no reason he would not be able to get his parents' attention tonight. Uncle Dennis had just gotten into his pickup and was driving away. He waved good-bye to Joey.

Then, out of the corner of his eye, Joey saw a five dollar bill float through the air. It seemed to come right out of the window of Uncle Dennis's pickup. That must be the five dollar bill he had seen his dad lay on the seat for the

gasoline. He ran to get it. He started to run into the house to show his father, but he stopped. If he had that five dollars plus his grandmother's three, he'd have plenty of money for his pumpkin seed. Besides, who could be sure where that bill came from! Joey put it into his pocket. All the joy that had been bubbling up in him was gone. Joey knew why, but he didn't admit it to himself. He had always been super honest. His father often talked to Joey about it. He said Joey had *integrity*. Joey had always been proud of that good sounding word when it was applied to him.

Now Joey wondered. Was his integrity gone? Was he willing to trade his integrity for a five dollar bill so he could buy pumpkin seed?

Joey didn't even try to talk about his project at the dinner table. Knowing that money was in his pocket caused him not to be able to speak freely. He kept feeling in his pocket to see if it were still there. He wished it would suddenly disappear so that he could go back to being a happy, excited boy with a pumpkin seed problem. He knew he should go to the telephone and call his uncle, but instead he went into his room and slipped the bill between two pages of the largest book he could find. He felt like a thief. He wondered why. He hadn't stolen that money.

Joey had many opportunities to talk to his parents that weekend. Weekends were always lazy days for his family. There was no pushing a time schedule. They always went to Sunday School and church on Sunday morning, but they didn't seem as rushed as they did on other days.

Joey let that weekend go by without saying a word about a 4-H project, about pumpkin seed, or about a five dollar bill which had come floating through the air.

The 4-H Club adviser came to school on Monday. Every kid in the club except Joey handed in his or her project plans.

"What's wrong, Joey?" the adviser asked. "I can't believe you aren't going to be trying for one of our prizes. You've always been our best competitor."

Joey replied that he needed to talk to him privately.

"OK," the adviser said. "But you'll have to come into my office in town. I'll be at another school this afternoon, and I'm already late. Come in any day after school."

Joey forgot that he didn't have a way to get to town and that by the time his mother and dad got home, the office would be closed. He had lost his enthusiasm to know more about albino pumpkins, for more pumpkin growing know-how, for anything. He just didn't have a single good feeling about himself. He really didn't like Joey McClintock! He had never felt like this before. He didn't like anyone or anything!

Suddenly Joey realized that Mrs. Kellogg was talking very excitedly about an author of children's books who was coming to town the next Saturday. She was a famous author of horse stories. Mrs. Kellogg said it would be like meeting an old friend for the children who had read any of her books. There was time to read one before Saturday if children got busy today.

Mrs. Kellogg had a large stack of books on her desk. She told the students a little about each book and sort of auctioned them off, as she explained that Marguerite Henry wrote about horses because she loved them. The teacher said the Henry books were filled with real, live horses and real, live people.

Joey was interested in every book Mrs. Kellogg talked about, but someone else always seemed to get his hand into the air first. Mrs. Kellogg was very fair. The person who got his hand up first got the book, but Joey got so interested in the story the teacher was telling that he forgot to raise his hand until someone else snatched up the book.

He watched all the books get away. He would have enjoyed any or all of them. *Misty; Misty of Chincoteague; Brighty of the Grand Canyon; Mustang; King of the Wind;*—what wonderful stories! Joey just knew his mother would go with him to meet Mrs. Henry.

When school was over, Joey hurried to the school bus.

How he wished he had gotten one of those books to read. He wondered why he had been so slow about getting his hand in the air.

He sat down in the back of the bus. Even with the bus full of noisy kids, Joey felt alone. Maybe, when he got home, he would feel better. At last the bus stopped at the turnoff to Joey's house. As he came down the aisle of the bus, he spotted a book lying in one of the seats. *Brighty of the Grand Canyon.* That was *the* one he had wanted most of all. Joey reached down and picked up the book. He put it with his things. The driver didn't notice. Joey knew he should have told her he found the book and that she would take it back to school, but he didn't. He just said, "Good-bye," and ran down the road to his home.

Joey hurried faster than usual through his chores. He went right to his room, turned on the light, and began to read.

He had never been to the Grand Canyon, but that was one of the places his parents said they were going on their vacation. How exciting it would be to see the places where Brighty and his friend "Old Timer" lived!

When his mother came home, Joey had read thirty pages. His mother was excited for him when he told her about the famous author who was coming to their town on Saturday. She asked him to tell her about the book he was reading. As Joey talked, his mother began to get out the pots and pans. He knew she was fixing dinner, but he wished she'd be quieter about it. He just wanted to read. Reading was his way of getting away from his problems. It was the only way he knew of getting totally away from everything. Reading was his magic carpet of escape.

But, when his mother called him to dinner and he laid down his book, his problem was still there—right in the pit of his stomach. Joey was a smart boy, and he knew that he had to face up to his problem. He had to handle it, and he had to have help to do that. He could just hear his father say, "When you've got a problem, lay it all out in the open. That's the only way to really solve it. As long as you keep part of it hidden, it will never be solved."

Joey's problem had to be solved. He just couldn't live with it or himself otherwise.

So, when the family sat down to Joey's favorite meal—spaghetti—he just barely waited until his daddy had said the blessing. Then he blurted out, "I've got a problem. It's a big, big problem. It's driving me crazy. I've got to have your help with it! Not tomorrow. Not the next day. I need help right now."

"All right, Son" comforted his dad, "don't upset yourself. We're right here. We're listening."

Joey couldn't believe his ears. They were both listening. He was so shocked and relieved that he began to cry. He hadn't really cried in a long, long time. Great sobs seemed to rise up from that tight spot in his stomach. His dad reached over and patted him on the back.

He said, "Whenever you feel like talking, your mother and I are ready to listen. You know, Son, I think you've been trying to talk to us for several days, and we've been too busy to listen. I think we owe you a great big, super-duper apology. I'm really sorry, Son, that we've been pushing you and your problem aside."

"That apology goes for me, too, Joey," his mother added. "I don't know what kept me from seeing that you needed help. Please forgive us, and let us help you now."

Joey didn't like cold spaghetti and his spaghetti was getting cold. But that didn't matter. He was going to talk about his problems.

"First, I'll talk about the pumpkin seed," he said. "That's what started the whole thing."

"Pumpkin seed?" his parents chorused.

"Yes, pumpkin seed," said the excited boy. "Let me show you." Joey ran into his room and brought the seed catalog back with him.

"I need pumpkin seed for a 4-H Club project," he explained. "Everybody else in the club has turned in his project except me. I couldn't turn mine in until I talked to you about seed. They are expensive, and so I don't know if

25

we can afford them. I know that the new car is stretching our budget, and I know that next summer's vacation is going to affect everything we do until then. But I still have to know if we can afford pumpkin seed."

The words just poured out of Joey's mouth. He did not slow down one bit.

"You see," he continued, "I guess I'm a little selfish. Mr. Billings says I'm his best competitor, and he wants me to get involved. But, the main thing is that I want to enter three contests. I've tried, but I can't be happy if I can't enter all three pumpkin contests."

"What do you want us to do to help you, Joey?" asked his mother.

"I need help with money. I need help ordering seed. I need help with getting a place to plant my seed. *And* I need help with 'know-how' about planting pumpkins."

"Oh, pumpkins aren't hard to grow," his dad said casually.

"These might be," Joey suggested. "You see, I want to win three prizes, and you don't win three prizes without doing something special."

"I think you're right, Son," his mother spoke out, "and I like your attitude. If you are going to enter a contest, enter with the idea of winning. The idea of winning makes the hard work easier."

"Let me tell you what contests I want to enter," Joey said, "then you can see if we can afford it. I want to enter the biggest pumpkin contest. That may be the hardest contest because people around here grow some mighty big pumpkins."

"Maybe Mr. Billings can tell you how to grow big pumpkins. He should know what seed would be best," commented Joey's dad.

"The second contest I want to enter is the ugliest jack-o'-lantern contest. I think I can win that one because I'm the best art student in the county if the past three years' county fairs prove anything. I'll just have to start with an odd, ugly shaped pumpkin—that'll be the way to win that contest."

"You've named only two contests. What's the other one?" Joey's mother's voice showed that she was getting excited.

"The other contest is the most unusual pumpkin contest. That's the one I'd like to win most of all. You see, I've got a great idea. I want to enter an albino pumpkin," announced Joey in a high-pitched voice.

"An albino pumpkin?" laughed his dad. "Joey, I think you've got the wrong word. Do you know what the word *albino* means?"

"I surely do, and I'm so glad you asked. It gives me an opportunity to explain to you that an albino pumpkin is a white-skinned pumpkin that originally came from Africa. It is very rarely grown in the United States. A few farmers grow it for novelty decorations for parties and business. I want to call mine 'ghost pumpkins.' You see, it's such a special idea I can't talk to anyone about it. I don't want any copycats. I don't want any albino competition. But you and Mom have to know that albino pumpkin seed are very expensive. Ten seed cost a dollar and a half, and I'm afraid that just ten seed would not be enough."

"Would twenty be enough?" asked his Mom.

"I think so. That would mean I could plant four hills with five seed in each hill. Mr. Billings taught me that you call each hole you dig for planting a hill," Joey explained.

"Well," said Joey's dad. "If I count right just using my head, that would come to $4.71, including tax but no postage. We should be able to get you going for $5.00."

"I have three dollars we can use," Joey volunteered.

"You do. Where did you get three dollars?" His mother's voice showed surprise.

"From my sweet, California grandma for April Fool's Day," Joey said. "I tried to tell you about it. You know my grandmother would never forget me, and she would never be late on April Fool's. *And* she knows I'd never, ever, ever

27

like anything better than folding money.''

Joey hurried to his room and brought back the money and his April Fool's card. ''Here is my investment in the pumpkin seed,'' he said. ''May we please order them tonight?''

''OK, Son,'' his dad said. ''Let's tear the order form from the seed catalog.''

Joey quickly tore out the form. His father said: ''Son, I'm glad we've talked about your problem, but I'm still a little confused. I don't understand why you were so upset. Is there, or was there, something else bothering you? If so, now's the time to lay all your cards on the table.''

''Well,'' Joey hedged.

''Well,'' echoed his father.

Joey continued, ''There is a little something else, but I don't know how to explain it.''

''Try,'' his father encouraged.

''I'll be back in a minute,'' Joey murmured as he left the room.

He returned with an envelope in his hand. On the outside was printed ''To: Anyone Who Finds This.'' He gave the envelope to his dad. There were dirty smudges on the outside of the envelope and a small amount of black soil in one corner.

''I didn't steal it,'' said Joey. ''I've still got my integrity. I found it.''

''You found this five dollar bill in this envelope?'' his dad questioned him.

''No. It wasn't in that envelope,'' Joey mumbled.

''You put it in the envelope?'' his father asked.

''Yes'' Joey whispered. ''I found the money outside, but I knew it blew out the window of Uncle Dennis's truck. At first, I was just waiting until he mentioned losing it. I hid it in a book. But I didn't like having it in my room—it bothered my integrity. And it bothered me. So, I put it in the envelope. We have to ask Uncle Dennis if he lost the five dollars you laid on the front seat of his pickup for gaso-

line the day we went fishing and the wind came up so fast.''

Joey's father sighed a great, big sigh. "Son, you don't know what a load you've lifted off my shoulders. We've always talked about honesty and integrity, and I've always felt that you understood and believed what we said. But when that five dollars disappeared and Uncle Dennis and I knew you were the only one around—well, my pride was hurt and my faith in my son was damaged.''

"I'm sorry, Dad,'' Joey said. "But you see, I was wrong because I was trying to figure out a way to keep that money I knew wasn't mine. I knew it was somebody else's, and I was almost sure it was Uncle Dennis's. I just kept trying to find a way to spend it for my pumpkin seed. I knew we were having money problems.''

"What do you think we should do now that we've got your order filled out?'' asked his father.

"I think I should call Uncle Dennis and explain that I have his five dollars. Do you think he'll believe me?'' Joey questioned.

"I think so,'' said his dad. "But it really is unimportant what he thinks. What is important is Joey McClintock's integrity and his father's faith in him. It's important, Joey, that a boy can believe in his father's integrity and that a father can believe in his son's integrity. My son has been put through a hard test, and he had come through it with a stamp of honesty upon him. I couldn't be a prouder, happier man tonight.''

"And I'm glad not to have that five dollars in my room. I'm flat broke, but I don't care. I'll go right now and call Uncle Dennis,'' Joey said.

Uncle Dennis listened to Joey's explanation about the five dollars. He was glad Joey was honest. Uncle Dennis told Joey to use the whole five dollars to buy albino pumpkin seed.

"I want you to have a lot of ghost pumpkins to choose from,'' Uncle Dennis had said. "I've never heard of albino pumpkins, but the whole idea sounds so crazy, I think you'll win. A boy who has integrity and who is industrious enough to enter three contests should be able to grow ghost pumpkins if anyone can."

Joey came back into the room to tell his father that he would have to remake the order for five dollars more. Uncle Dennis believed in Joey's integrity too!

After church on Sunday, Joey and his father took a walk across the uncultivated land behind their house. They talked about the soil, water supply, and protection during the harvesting season. Joey, who hadn't thought of anything except planting his seed, was glad to have his father's advice and help. Now he could write up his projects, get a statement from his father that he should be permitted to ride the school bus to town to see Mr. Billings, mail his seed order, and go to work digging his hills. His father told him to take notes when Mr. Billings explained.

Mr. McClintock continued, "You think you'll remember everything he says, but you won't, so write your instructions down step by step. You can work hard all summer long, but water too much or too little at the wrong time could spoil everything."

Mr. Billings was pleased when Joey showed up at his office on Monday afternoon after school. Joey explained the three projects he had planned. The one which pleased Mr. Billings most was the albino project.

"Joey," he said, "if you didn't have that seed catalog, I would just think that I had a kid with a wild imagination on my hands. White pumpkins! Ghost pumpkins! Young man, I get excited just thinking about the stir you are going to create at the county fair next fall. I probably know as much about agriculture as anyone around and I've never heard of albino pumpkins. Let's keep your project as our secret. You don't want anyone else horning in on it. Tell your parents that mum's the word. Now follow these directions in digging each one of your hills, and I'll drive out to your house next Saturday to talk with your father about the planting. I'm leaving on vacation in a couple of weeks. Your seed should arrive before I get back, and they should be planted as soon as they arrive. Would you promise me one thing?

"Save one of the albino seed," Mr. Billings continued, "until I get back so that I can see it before you plant it. Ghost pumpkins! What fun I could have had with an albino pumpkin patch when I was a kid!"

"Mr. Billings, could I ask my Uncle Dennis to come on Saturday too? He's sort of like my partner. He has five dollars invested in my seed. He won't tell anyone anything. He's really a neat man for a grown-up!"

"Sure, Joey. It's your project," Mr. Billings answered. "Your Uncle Dennis is welcome. Tell your father to call me if it is not all right for me to come around 10:30 on Saturday. I'll write the time and my telephone number at home on the front of this envelope filled with pumpkin planting information. By the way, I must say how pleased I am that you thought of a way to get into town today. I'll have to share your thinking with other kids who need to talk to me about their projects. What you have just done proves that old saying, 'Where there's a will, there's a way!' You've certainly proved that necessity is the mother of invention."

"I don't quite understand what that last sentence means," Joey said as he squirmed from foot to foot.

"That just means that when a person has a problem, if he puts his mind to it, he'll think of a way to solve it. He'll invent a way if necessary. You got to town by thinking of riding the bus. Now I'll share your invention, how to get to town, with kids all over the county. Do you understand?"

"Sure. I'll go home tonight and tell my mother that I became a mother today through necessity. She's really going to crack up! I can just hear her say, 'My son, Joey McClintock is a mother. Does that make me a grandmother—of invention that is?"

Joey looked at the big wall clock. Mr. Billings glanced at it too. "Your mother said for you to come to her office before five, so you need to hurry over there."

32

"Good-bye, Mr. Billings. Thanks for everything. I'll see you Saturday at 10:30," shouted the happy, would-be pumpkin farmer as he ran quickly from the room.

Saturday was a beautiful Kansas spring morning. Joey was up early. He ate a big breakfast of pancakes and sausage and then ran outside to wait for his uncle Dennis to arrive. Finally his mother called to him: "Joey, come in and clean your room. Mr. Billings won't be here for another hour and a half. The time will pass faster if you're busy. You know that old saying: 'A watched pot never boils!' "

"OK," Joey yelled to her, "but first I'm going to check the mailbox. I just saw the mailcarrier put something in it."

"Don't get your hopes up too high. It's been only one week since we sent off the order," his mother cautioned.

Joey was back from the mailbox in a few minutes.

"False alarm," he murmured as he came in. "But you'll like what the mailcarrier left. It's a new spring and summer catalog. Now you can start your summer wishing."

At long last Joey heard a car drive up, and he ran outside to greet his uncle Dennis. Right behind Uncle Dennis came Mr. Billings. Joey liked it when people kept their appointments. It made everything go more smoothly.

"Good morning," Joey called. "I'm really excited about planting my pumpkins, but the seed haven't come yet. My mom says that I haven't given the seed company enough time."

"Don't fret, Joey," Mr. Billings spoke softly to the boy. "You've got days and days of work ahead of you before you plant your seed."

"Days and days of work?" Joey's voice showed his surprise.

"Yes, days and days. Digging the holes and preparing them for planting will be the hardest work you've ever

33

done. I'm glad your dad and uncle Dennis are here because you are going to need someone to keep encouraging you when your project bogs down in the middle."

"My project isn't going to bog down in the middle. I've waited too long to get my pumpkin seed to let that happen," Joey answered enthusiastically.

Joey's dad came in from the backyard. "Good morning," he greeted everyone. "Are you ready to look over our prospective pumpkin patch?"

"You bet," Uncle Dennis affirmed. "I'm almost as anxious as Joey to get this show on the road."

At first Mr. Billings just looked at the area. Then he said, "Your soil isn't very good. It will take a lot of building up to raise anything except crabgrass. But with enough fertilizer and water, Joey should be able to get some good pumpkins.

"This is going to be hard digging," continued Mr. Billings. "The ground doesn't look like it has ever been cultivated, and the grass roots are as thick as can be. Your hills should be about eight feet apart, so we should cut as many stakes as you want hills and stake it out first. Then the hard work begins. Let's dig our first hill right here."

Joey and his dad got a shovel and began digging. Mr. Billings explained to Joey that the crabgrass had to go, roots and all. "Once that crabgrass gets water, it will grow like wildfire, so we have to wipe it all out."

"Can't we just use some kind of weed-killer?" Joey questioned.

"Sure thing," Mr. Billings drawled, "but your weed-killer might kill your pumpkins too."

"Oops, hadn't thought of that. I guess that, like it or not, I've just got to dig out that grass."

"Now you get the message. Joey, farming is a hard business, but when harvesttime comes, it seems worth all the labor. I just want you to know that raising pumpkins or anything else worthwhile is not like mixing instant breakfast. It doesn't happen easily. It's more like a good stew

that your mother puts in a slow cooker to cook all day while she's at work.

"You see that stew won't be any good if she doesn't put in the good things to start with. Do you remember the stone soup story when you were smaller? Everybody knew that you couldn't make stone soup, but everybody put his best ingredients into it and a good soup resulted. If we put our best into this pumpkin patch, we'll get good pumpkins. But if we prepare poor hills, not deep enough or wide enough; if we skimp on fertilizer, fail to water enough and at the right time; or fail to pinch off the excess blooms, we won't get the best pumpkins. It's just that simple."

"How deep should this hill be and how wide?" asked Joey's dad.

"At least two feet square and at least a foot deep. Here, Joey, let's have you dig a hill all by yourself. I'll time you so that you will have some idea of how long this project is going to take."

Joey listened carefully. He was very quiet because he was thinking. "This pumpkin growing is going to be a serious matter and lots of hard work." He dug away at his hill. It was hard digging. His father went to the garage and came back with a hatchet and an axe. He gave Joey the hatchet because of its short handle.

"I think these will help us cut away the grass so that we can dig into the soil," he said. "I was getting nowhere."

"Neither was I," Joey agreed. "This is much better."

The three men talked about vacations, fishing, the lack of a rainy spring season, and finally came back to Joey's pumpkin patch. About thirty-five minutes had passed when Mr. Billings came over to examine Joey's hole. "Looks about right," he said. "You might deepen it about three inches."

"That much?" said Joey, but he kept on digging. He wanted it done just right, and he wanted to please all the men.

"That's enough," Mr. Billings finally said in a few minutes. "Joey, I would allow an hour's time for each hole. You now have four holes to begin with. Plan how many holes you need to dig and decide how many you can dig each day. As soon as your dad can get the fertilizer, you need to start mixing it in with the soil. By the time your seeds arrive, you will be ready to plant them and that's going to be your happy day."

Joey was perspiring. The men were perspiring too. Joey said: "I'm going to the house to see if Mom has something cold for us to drink. We need it. That was hard work."

When Joey was out of earshot, Mr. Billings told Mr. McClintock that Joey would need lots of encouragement in the digging of the hills.

"Farming isn't a glamorous job. Daily appreciation of the progress Joey has made will help. Help him set up a daily goal. Don't let him undertake too much or he'll fizzle out. Defeat before the crop is planted often happens with our 4-H kids. They bite off more than they can chew. And because they have no adults to encourage them, they give up. Try to look at Joey's project every day. Don't do the work for him. This is Joey's idea, Joey's project, Joey's work, and Joey's joy. Your son will do a lot of growing up as he carries out his plans. I will come out to check on him as soon as my vacation is over."

Joey came back with lemonade and glasses. "I drank two full glasses," he said. "Boy, is it good!"

The men finished the pitcher of lemonade, then Mr. Billings and Uncle Dennis left. Joey and his father sat down in the middle of the pumpkin patch to plan their work strategy. Joey was happy to have his father's help.

"It's like playing games," Joey said. "If you don't plan and don't think as you play, you lose. This is one game I surely don't want to lose."

"What is our first step?" asked his dad.

"We have to stake off our patch. Do you have any

wood we can use for that?'' Joey asked.

"I think so. Let's look in the garage. Bring your hatchet. We may need it," replied Mr. McClintock.

Joey and his dad soon had the stakes cut for thirty pumpkin hills. Then they staked them off.

"That was the easy part," said Joey. "Now begins the *drudgery*. After digging only one hole, I know what that word means. Dad, I think I'll dig another hole now. It should go a little faster this time. I'll know a little more about digging."

"Good idea," said his dad. "I'll dig another hole too. Then we'll go to town and get the fertilizer. We want to do this just right."

"You mean we can afford to buy fertilizer today? I didn't say anything to Mr. Billings because I was afraid we couldn't afford that just now. I thought we might have to wait until next month."

The two hills were soon dug and Joey was pleased.

"That's six of them," Joey exclaimed. "Only twenty-four more to go. I must go clean up. I'm sure Mom wouldn't want me to go to town like this. But I can be ready in a few minutes."

The fertilizer cost $4.67. Joey wrote that figure down in his project booklet. Next fall when he sold his pumpkins he intended to pay his dad back. One thing he had already learned from his pumpkin patch was that farming is expensive. He guessed that he had always thought that farming was free.

The next day at church, Joey had a lot for which to be thankful. He couldn't talk about his plans to grow albino pumpkins. But he could thank God silently, and he did. He was seated between his parents, and he did something he would never have thought of doing before. He reached out and took hold of their hands and squeezed them. He knew they would know what he meant. He had had such a happy week that he wanted God and his parents to know how grateful he was.

On Monday after school, Joey hurried home. He and his father had decided that he should dig at least two holes each day. He changed into his work clothes, drank a glass of milk, and ate two brownies.

"Work, work, work, here I come," he hummed to himself as he picked up his tools and headed for the backyard and his pumpkin patch.

He worked hard. Soon he had dug his first hole. The second went more slowly.

"I think I'm tired, but I must have this done when Dad gets home. Then he can help me mix the fertilizer in. After today, I can do everything myself."

When he finished digging the second hole, he threw himself down on the grass.

"Rest, rest, rest, that's what I need. I'll just lie here for awhile, then I'll go get myself a good drink of lemonade."

Joey made a big pitcher of lemonade. He drank his fill, then spoke aloud to himself.

"Joey, old boy, that sun is still way up there. You could dig another hole today and be one ahead of your schedule. Or you could watch TV. How about it, Joey?"

Joey went back out to his hole digging. He didn't know what it was down inside him which caused him to do it, but he knew he was right in doing so. He also knew that his dad would be pleased if he did more than his schedule demanded. It was like doing an extra page of arithmetic or a column of bonus words in spelling. Joey liked doing more than was required of him in anything he undertook. It always made him feel good inside. He didn't know why, but it did.

His dad drove up just as Joey finished his third hole. He ran to meet him, yelling as he got close, "Dad, I did three holes today. Isn't that great? Now I'm ready for the fertilizer."

"OK, I'll carry the sack out. You go in the kitchen and bring out Mom's big two-cup measure. Mr. Billings said we need two cups for each hill."

Joey ran into the house and back out by the time his dad got to the pumpkin patch. Joey didn't seem to be tired any more. It didn't take him very long to put nine big measuring cups of fertilizer on his nine hills. Then he began mixing the dirt and fertilizer. Was he ever getting dirty! His dad was mixing with the shovel. He wasn't getting dirty at all. Joey decided his dad's way was better. He knew his mother wasn't going to like his dirty clothes, but he would tell her that he wouldn't get that dirty again.

When they were finished, they walked back to the house. His mother had come home, and they could smell pork chops cooking as soon as they opened the door.

"Joey McClintock, what on earth have you been doing to get so dirty?" His mother's high voice showed her annoyance. "Here, Daddy, take this broom and him outside, and get as much of that dirt off of him as possible. Then strip him down to his undershorts and leave those clothes on the back porch. Now hurry. I'll run water in the bathtub. Supper will be ready in fifteen minutes."

"I'll be ready in fourteen minutes," Joey said. "I wasn't hungry until I got my first whiff of those pork chops. Please make some of my favorite gravy to go with them."

A very clean Joey soon emerged from the bathroom. Because he was very tired, he had dressed in clean pajamas.

"I'm going right to bed after dinner. I'm really tired," he said.

"Mom, you're going to be proud of Joey," said his father. "He did two pumpkin hills plus one, and he mixed all the fertilizer into the soil. But he won't get that dirty again. He can use that small camping shovel to mix the fertilizer. He just got carried away in his mixing."

"Did you get carried away with cleaning the tub?" asked his mother.

"Oops, I'm afraid I didn't, but I will as soon as I get through eating. My nose has been leading me to the table for the last thirteen minutes. Will that gravy be ready in a minute, Mom?''

"Yes, I think so. With you men so hungry, this food should really hit the spot. I've heard that's what makes food really good."

Nine days later Joey came home from school tired, irritable, and out of sorts with himself. He had not gotten along well with his friends at school that day, but he didn't know why. He did know that he didn't want to dig any pumpkin holes. So he didn't even go out to his patch. He just sprawled out on the living room floor, turned the TV to his favorite after-school program, and was soon sound asleep. He didn't hear his mother come in. He didn't hear his dad drive up. He just heard his mom when she called to him to get washed up for dinner.

"Supper is a little early tonight," his mom said. "I had lots of food left over from that dinner at the church yesterday, so we're just having warmed up leftovers. But, oh, what good leftovers!"

Joey rubbed his eyes and the back of his neck. He still didn't feel well, but he didn't mention it.

"Well, Son, how did things go today?" asked his father.

"Not so hot," Joey murmured.

"You're almost through with your digging, aren't you?" asked his father.

Joey met the problem head on. "I didn't dig any today," he said. "I didn't want to. I didn't feel like it. I was too tired. I just didn't care if I got behind my schedule. Besides, what good is it going to do to have thirty holes dug if my seed never come. Every day I get more and more disappointed when I open the mailbox."

"I can see how you get disappointed," his mother said. "But remember the agreement you and your dad made—no seed-planting until all the holes are dug. What if your seed come tomorrow? That's possible, you know."

Joey's dad didn't say anything for awhile. When he did speak, he said: "I understand your disappointment in your seed not coming. I'm disappointed too. But tomorrow is another day, and your seed might come then.''

Joey ran from the school bus to the mailbox the next day. When he pulled down the front of the box to look inside, his heart was pounding wildly. He wasn't disappointed. The box was stuffed with a package from the seed company. Joey was delighted, but there was no one to share his excitement. He hurried into the living room, opened the package, checked to see that everything was included, then scolded himself: "Joey, you really goofed up yesterday. Because you didn't work yesterday, you can't get all your holes dug today. But you can get busy and do as much as possible. Get into your work clothes.''

Joey dug hard and fast, but the digging was getting harder every day. His dad said it was because there had been no rain for over a month. When he had dug two hills, he sat down and sighed:

"Only two more to go, but I'm so tired I don't think I can dig two more. How about one, Joey? If you dig one more, then you'll be able to finish early tomorrow; and maybe you can plant your seed.''

A car roared into his driveway, but Joey didn't stop digging. He had caught his old enthusiasm once again. When his Uncle Dennis called out to him, he was so surprised he jumped. He didn't know anyone was near.

"Hi, Uncle Dennis. Guess what! My seed came today. I'm really excited about planting them, but my dad says I have to have all my holes dug before I can start planting.''

Uncle Dennis walked over and picked up the shovel Joey's father had used on the first digging day.

"Here,'' he said, "Let me give you a hand. I'm stronger than you are. With the two of us working, it shouldn't take us too long to dig a pumpkin hill.''

The digging went much, much faster than when Joey dug alone.

"Uncle Dennis, I'll be glad when I'm as big and strong as you are. Just think how hard I can throw a baseball when I'm that strong!''

"Only one more hole," said Uncle Dennis when hole number twenty-nine was dug.

"Aunt Suzie will be unhappy with me for being late for dinner, but I need to talk with your dad before work tomorrow. Since he isn't here yet, let's start hole number thirty."

Joey liked Uncle Dennis's help, but he was so tired he could hardly think about beginning another hole. He got his hatchet and began cutting away the grass.

"Here, Joey, let me do that," said his uncle. "You look all tuckered out. Why don't you go into the house and call Aunt Suzie? Tell her that I'm going to be about thirty minutes late for dinner."

When Joey got back outside, his Uncle Dennis had almost finished hole number thirty. Joey couldn't believe it.

"Here, Uncle Dennis," he volunteered. "Let me do the digging. I want to dig out the last shovelful. It looks to me like you're almost down to it. You surely are good to help me. I'm glad you are so interested in my pumpkins and me."

A few minutes later Joey yelled: "That's it! Hole number thirty, you are finished! Joey, old boy, when you have mixed four big cups of fertilizer into your soil, you will be ready to plant your seed."

It was nearly dark. Joey didn't even suggest that they plant the seed. As lightweight as the seed were, Joey didn't think he could lift even one of them, let alone plant a hill.

"I'll ask my dad to help me plant one hill before I go to bed tonight," he said. "Then I'll know how to plant the other twenty-nine tomorrow. I get excited just thinking about it."

Uncle Dennis finally had to go home without seeing Joey's dad. Joey was alone. He sat down on the living room floor and looked at his seed again. A lot of wonderful ideas were whirling around in his head. Some people might call them wide-awake dreams, but Joey knew they would stay with him until the county fair and the pumpkin contest.

Deep down in his heart Joey felt that he would be a winner. He stretched out on the floor, glad to be able to rest for awhile. He did not wake up until his mom called him to get ready for dinner. He could smell something tantalizing. Was it pineapple upside-down cake? That was one of his favorite desserts.

"Son, how did the hole-digging go today?" asked his dad.

"I'm finished, all finished. You can't imagine my good luck. Uncle Dennis came by to see you, and he helped me with holes twenty-nine and thirty. He can dig twice as fast as I can. So I'm through—through—through, and I'm happy—happy—happy."

After dinner, Joey and his father sat down and read the planting instructions step by step. Then they got a light and went out to hill number one. Joey carried a three-gallon bucket of water.

"Might as well break you in right," said his father. "You'll be carrying a lot of water this summer."

The planting didn't take long, but that was only one hill. Multiply that by thirty and that's a long time. Then there was the water. Joey noticed that the soil just swallowed the three gallons of water immediately. His dad explained that everyone in their part of Kansas was worried about the long dry spell. "There's talk of water rationing in town, but we've got our trusty, old well so we shouldn't suffer."

"What about my pumpkins? Will they suffer?" asked a worried Joey.

"We hope not. We've come this far, and you've worked so hard that we're going to fight for your project. There's water in Lake Redman. We can always haul some in if we have to."

Joey had decided on planting his albino pumpkins as far away from the house as he could. Casual visitors to their home wouldn't be apt to see them out there. The albino project was his great, big, wonderful secret. Tomorrow he would get those seed in the soil.

The next day at noon there was a tornado alert in the area. School let out early. The students were told to contact their parents immediately if they were away from home. The bus driver drove faster than usual, so Joey got home and had called his mother by 2:30. She told him to open the cellar door and stay there waiting for her unless the wind began to blow. In that case, he was to go into the cellar and close the door.

Joey's mom was home in fifteen minutes. She had driven faster than usual. The tornado alert had changed to a tornado watch, so she said he could plant his seed while she listened for the weather reports.

Joey wasn't happy about the tornado alert. All Kansas hated tornado season because of the damage and death the storms brought; but if there had to be an alert, he was glad his mom was home to listen so that he could plant. She got a portable radio and came out to his patch. The static was bad because of the lightning in the area, but they could hear that the storm was north of them.

It took Joey an hour to plant his albino seed. Carrying the water was the biggest job. His mother carried two hoses from the garage, hooked them together, and brought the water 125 feet closer than the back door. Joey really smiled when she did that.

"First Daddy helped me then Uncle Dennis, and now you," he said. "I'm really lucky to belong to my family. We're all working on this pumpkin project. I guess we'll have to have a pumpkin pie party when we're through raising pumpkins."

By the time Joey's dad got home, the tornado alert had been over for an hour, but Joey's mother had said they would not be going to the weekly prayer service at the church.

"We'll just do our praying here," said his father. "There is no cellar at the church, and the tornado watch is still on."

When they sat down to dinner, Joey asked if he might be the one to say the blessing.

"I just have so much to be grateful for," he said, "that I'm afraid I'll pop if I don't get to tell God about it soon."

After the blessing, Joey's father explained to Joey that he needn't wait until mealtime or bedtime to pray—that God was available all the time—that he could have prayed as he planted.

"Oh, I know that," said Joey. "But praying at those times seems doubly good, maybe more important—not just like wishing or dreaming. That's why I wanted to pray tonight."

"You have made a good point, Son," agreed Mr. McClintock. "I think it's like our Thanksgiving prayer service. If we make the effort to go to the church to pray at that time, it seems more meaningful. But tonight I think the Lord would expect us to stay at home where we are safe. We can have a special prayertime just before we go to bed."

Every day and night for the next few days there were tornado watches and alerts. The whole countryside was uneasy. The children still went to school, but by noon the bus was usually rambling down the road to take them home.

It was hot, dry weather. Joey's mother brought work home from the office to do. Other women did the same. They talked on the phone about problems, and Joey saw something he had never noticed before. The adults didn't try to get out of work when a problem arose—they tried to find a way to work around the problem. He must remember that in the pumpkin business. If the drought continued, he and his father would have to find extra water. Lake Redman seemed the best place to him, and that was ten miles away. He wondered where they could get barrels big enough to make a trip pay off. He needed to talk to his father about that.

On Friday night, Joey blurted out his problem at the dinner table.

"Dad," he said as he wiggled in his seat. "I'm wor-

48

ried about barrels to haul my pumpkin water in if our water gets rationed."

"I'm worried too," answered his dad. "Uncle Dennis has one barrel, and I have one. We need at least four barrels and should have six if we are to make a trip pay. Tomorrow, we'll drive into town and see what we can find. We'll go by all our relatives, and we'll ask our friends."

"That's a relief to my mind," Joey stated. "Just knowing you are worried, too, helps me a lot. It's like that prayer thing. When I know other people are praying too, it seems to give me and my prayers strength."

They found a good barrel at Joey's great-uncle's. He said he wouldn't be using it unless things got desperate because he had two. They found two very oily barrels at a filling station. Since they were metal, Joey's dad said they could burn them clean. The last find was an old wooden barrel. Its staves had all fallen apart, but his dad seemed sure that he could get it back to where it would hold water. Joey didn't believe it would, but this project had taught him a big lesson. Adults knew lots of things which kids didn't know. This might be another one of them!

Mr. McClintock and Joey filled the two oily barrels with firewood and trash when they got home. Then they rolled them to a safe place and set them afire. They burned and burned. The oil was thick and gave off lots of smoke and heat.

"We may have to fill them again another day," his dad said. "But that fire will do the job."

Next he asked Joey to fill one of the good barrels with water. Then he carefull put the staves and the end of the old barrel down in the water. "They will soak up water for the next few days; and when I put them together, they will stay together. Barrel makers have done that for centuries. I don't believe that any of the staves are missing. How about it, Son? Do you think you've worked enough today? Let's see what your mother is up to!"

Joey's mother was "up to" cooking a good meal. She had invited Aunt Suzie and Uncle Dennis. That meant he would have Micah and Rachel to play with. He must remember not to tease them just because he was bigger than they were. It had been too good a day to ruin with teasing, so he got out games to play that gave no opportunity for anything but a good time. He decided that he was learning to be responsible.

As the days passed, Joey's seed began to come through the ground.

"I think I feel like a mother hen whose eggs have just hatched," laughed Joey. "I can hardly wait until I get home from school to see how much my 'babies' have grown each day. I know that the seed books said I must cull them out, that I must throw lots of them away, two thirds of them. How, oh how, will I ever be able to do that? What if I throw some away and the others don't grow? I guess a real farmer just has to develop some faith in himself, his seed, the weather, and God. I'll talk to my dad about it tonight."

Joey's father told him to give the plants another week of growing. He was glad about that, but when the time came for the big decision, it was much harder than he had expected. The plants were bigger, prettier, and more sturdy. But he finally did it. He knew he had to! The notation in his project journal read: "Today I carefully removed the extra plants from each hill. I could hardly do it, but I knew I must. My hills look very vacant."

Joey's plants began to grow by leaps and bounds. Because of the intense hot weather, he watered half of them each day. Each Saturday he and his father drove to Lake Redman to get their six barrels of water. It was not such a hard task loading the water, but getting those barrels unloaded was very hard. They had to make a ramp to do it, and they often spilled some of the water. Joey's dad had to have the truck for work each day so they had to unload it, like it or not.

The pumpkin vines soon covered the whole pumpkin patch. When they began to bloom, Joey had to wrestle with a big decision. The book said to leave no more than three to five blooms on each plant—less for the really big pumpkins—and some of his plants already had ten or more blooms.

His father came to his rescue. "Try to space them well," he advised. "It seems only right that each pumpkin has an equal amount of vine."

That sounded sensible to Joey. As long as the blooms were big and healthy looking, he chose them in that manner.

Now all the decisions had been made. Joey asked his mother for fifteen big grocery sacks as soon as his pumpkins measured five inches across. He cut the sacks in halves and put them under the pumpkins. That would give him nice clean pumpkins without mildew on the bottoms. He read the directions again and again. He felt sure he had left no "unturned stones," and he was happy.

Gradually, Joey began to relax. His pumpkins would either make it or not. He had done his best. The Fourth of July would soon be here, and he was going to have a good time on that grand and glorious day.

Everything was going fine with Joey's pumpkins until the day of the big hailstorm. Hailstorms are not unusual in Kansas, but that hailstorm was. Some of the stones were as large as lemons and grapefruit. None were smaller than golf balls, it seemed.

The yard and Joey's pumpkin patch looked like a big bed of snowballs. The storm lasted only a few minutes, but it did much damage to roofs and crops. Joey was very disturbed because he knew that his pumpkin vines would be damaged. He hoped that his pumpkins would not be. As soon as the storm stopped, he ran out to check. He removed as many of the icy hailstones as he could as fast as he could. They melted quickly because the soil was so warm. That helped a lot, but Joey could see bruises on the

51

leaves of the plants. He did not notice much damage to the pumpkins. He knew he would have to wait a few days for bruises to show up there.

About a week later when Joey went out to water his plants, he noticed that two of the vines were almost totally wilted, so he gave them lots of extra water. He wondered if he had accidentally overlooked them the day before. He had always been careful not to skip any of the plants.

The next afternoon Joey really became upset. The two plants which were wilted the day before were now dead, and two more plants were wilted. Joey was crushed. Water was not his problem. He decided to call Mr. Billings. Joey was really in luck. Mr. Billings had some unscheduled time that afternoon and said he would drive out to take a look. Joey sat down on the front doorstep to wait. He was really feeling low when Mr. Billings arrived.

In a minute or two, Mr. Billings saw what was wrong. He picked up one of the vines.

"Gophers!" he said. "Joey, you've got a pesky gopher in your patch. We've got to get him before he cuts down all your plants."

"Gophers?" Joey said. "Where did they come from?"

"We'll probably never know, but here is the way he came to the patch. If we're lucky, there may be only one. Finding and killing one gopher can be very hard. Let's see what we can learn about this vandal. If we find him, he'll wish he had never decided to destroy your patch. The water you've been carrying probably caused him to come to your patch because there's no moisture elsewhere."

Mr. Billings asked Joey to sit down and to be very quiet. He did the same. Very soon the gopher made his presence known. His head peered over one of the dirt piles he had left behind. Joey got so excited that he squealed his delight and ran over to where Mr. Billings was sitting. But that brief moment gave the gopher all the warning he needed to make his retreat. Joey was terribly embarrassed. He had ruined their opportunity to try to hem in the crafty little animal.

Joey sputtered his apologies.

"Don't fret it," Mr. Billings said. "We weren't really ready for him anyway, but we must get ready. First, we'll bring out our axes and shovels. We've got to get him soon. Here's what we'll do the next time," he said as he outlined their next approach. The two of them left the patch to get equipment.

"I've seen farmers lose a whole garden to one gopher," Mr. Billings continued. "We can't afford to let that happen if we can possibly help it. Those little animals do a lot of damage at night; so I'm sure he'll be back as soon as he feels we are gone."

When Mr. McClintock got home, Joey and Mr. Billings were still watching for the gopher. But they had seen no more of him. Mr. Billings did not want to give up, but he had a meeting he had to attend. Joey's dad listened to the plan and took over.

Time passed very slowly for Joey and his dad. Joey's mother called that dinner was ready. They left their vigil and went in to eat. Joey asked as they sat down, "Dad, is my gopher problem big enough for me to ask God's help in solving it?"

"Of course, Son, God is concerned about all your problems, but one thing you must remember—sometimes his answer is no!"

"But why would he want a gopher to destroy my pumpkin patch?" Joey asked.

"Oh, he doesn't want that. He just allows it to happen. God doesn't want people to have car wrecks, but he allows them to happen. We need to ask God to help us think of a way to stop that gopher. There are lots of ways God can help us," his father answered.

"That's a good idea," said Joey. "I'll just pray that we'll know exactly what to do next time we see that gopher *burrowing*. How do you like that word? Mr. Billings taught me about it today."

Joey and his dad went outside again as soon as they had helped clear away the dinner dishes. Mrs. McClintock walked out with them to see what was going on, but Joey took no chances of her scaring away or alerting the gopher. He made sure that she would not repeat his mistake.

They saw the gopher working away in the middle of the patch when they returned. Joey's dad stationed Joey where one tunnel led away from where the gopher was working. He could cut off retreat there. He laid the big axe nearby and went to the other side where the gopher was working. He began to dig. The gopher scuttled backwards. He might ordinarily be slow, but not then. He was in high gear. Joey cut off his exit. Now the little animal was caught between them. Furiously they dug toward each other being careful not to let him get away. Quickly they closed the distance between them. Joey felt sorry for the gopher, but not sorry enough to let him cut down all the pumpkin plants. After a short while, Joey's dad yelled, "I got him! I know I hit him, but he's gone now. My, he's a strong little guy."

Joey yelled, "He's coming toward me. Hurry, Dad. He can't get by me. I've got my shovel across his path.

Mr. McClintock grabbed the axe and cut the burrow. Quickly he repeated the action several times. "I think I got him that time. Poor little guy. He won't be able to survive many more blows. I'm going to dig down here. I think he's dead."

A moment later, he lifted a shovelful of dirt and gopher. The little vandal was dead—he would cut down no more pumpkin vines. Joey was sure they would not have caught him so quickly if the gopher had not been so young and inexperienced.

"Now," Joey beamed, "we can get back to being pumpkin farmers. How wonderful!"

The summer was a long, dry one. The drought was severe in Kansas and in the neighboring states. The McClintocks decided against taking a vacation. Joey's pumpkin patch could not have survived without water, and hauling the water from Lake Redman was a weekly affair. One could not ask someone else to take that on, plus watering the plants too.

Joey's project was a thriving one. The heat seemed good for the pumpkins. Joey felt proud and satisfied as he walked and worked in his field. He would have liked to be able to share it with his friends, but so many of them had given up their projects because of lack of rain that he would be afraid that his success might hurt their feelings. Besides, he wanted his albino pumpkins, his ghost pumpkins, to be a complete surprise at the county fair.

October arrived with a brisk, cold day. Joey was exuberant. It was only fifteen days until the county fair and the 4-H contest. He had already selected his contest pumpkins, and each day he checked on them. He was very pleased with all his plans. He had a big pumpkin which had an ugly, odd shape that he would enter in the jack-o'-lantern art contest. His entry would be so unusually different, it was bound to attract attention.

Joey's big pumpkin was a huge one, but he did not have any idea how big other kids' pumpkins had grown. It was the only pumpkin on one vine, a whole vine for one pumpkin. Last year there were many huge pumpkins. Would there be this year?

However, Joey's great pride and joy was his whole patch of albinos. The biggest one was not a huge pumpkin, but he had great hopes that it would be the most unusual pumpkin at the fair.

The day before the fair was to begin, Joey cut his pumpkins from the vines and brought them into the living room. He just couldn't wait any longer to make sure they were safe for the contest. When he got home from school, he spread out newspapers on the floor, sketched his design on the misshapen pumpkin with a piece of charcoal, and very carefully began to carve. As he carved, he felt very sure he would be a winner. His odd-shaped pumpkin was becoming a very scary jack-o'-lantern. Joey was happy as he worked. Art was his favorite activity, and this was his chance to let his artistic ideas show.

He finished the carving and cleaned up the mess before his parents got home. He was glad about that because he wanted to surprise them. He also wanted them to know that he was planning ahead—no last minute hurry-up and get-it-done for him. He put Mr. Ugly Scary Jack in the middle of the kitchen table. Oh, how wonderful the frightening thing was in a spooky way!

Joey saved the pumpkin seed. They were slimy and hard to handle, but he got them clean and spread them on a paper in the garage. He would ask his parents if he could roast the seed after they had time to dry out.

Everything was done. Joey was exhausted, but happy. He got down the calendar and counted the days that had passed since he first began to think pumpkin patch. Over 150 days! *And* he was still as keen on the idea as when he began! Did that mean he was growing up, that he was maturing? Even Joey could see that he had really assumed the responsibility for this project.

"Come on, Dad. Come on, Mom. I can't wait much longer for you to see my jack-o'-lantern. Oh, how I hope you like him."

At last his parents' car crept up the driveway. Joey could tell that something was wrong by the way they walked so slowly and talked to each other. A neighbor had been hurt in an accident, so they needed to eat quickly and go over to do his evening chores. But Mr. and Mrs. McClintock didn't let Joey down.

"Joey, what a jack-o'-lantern you've made," his mother happily commented. "I knew you would do a good job, but he's super!"

"Super-ugly scary, downright hideous!" laughed his dad. "He'll scare the judges away."

They ate sandwiches quickly and piled into the car. The neighbor did not live very far away, so it did not take long to get there. On the way, Joey's dad said, "Son, I'm really a proud dad tonight. Getting your pumpkins done early really helped out. Your mom was worried about how we would handle things this evening, but she need not have been. You handled them just right.''

Joey's dad milked the neighbor's two cows and put out feed for the next day for all the animals. Joey sat with the children while their mother tended to her husband's needs. Mrs. McClintock made a chocolate cake and prepared a casserole for the next day. In a couple of hours, they were ready to go home. Joey was glad. He was so tired that his bed seemed to be calling him.

Just before he dropped off to sleep, he called out to his parents, "Hey, you guys, thanks a million for all your help all these months. If I win tomorrow, it will be because God, you, Mr. Billings, Uncle Dennis, and Grandma helped me. I'm really sorry for kids whose parents don't encourage them."

The next day Joey had to fill out three entry blanks when they got to the 4-H building. Everyone was in a feverish excitement. Every kid wanted to win as much as Joey did. Somehow Joey had not sensed that excitement among his friends at school, but it was really noticeable here.

He wandered around listening for comments. He saw all the judges gathered around his albino pumpkin. Some of them were shaking their heads. Some were laughing at the white pumpkin. Some were cautiously sampling the white pumpkin pie which Joey's mother had made just to prove that the albino was a pumpkin.

"May look like a ghost," one judge said, "but the taste is the real thing. This is pumpkin pie for sure!"

Joey had a half day to wait. The prizes would not be announced until one o'clock. His hands and his brow were wet with sweat. He needed to do something to keep his mind off his entries. He decided to go to the livestock area. He always enjoyed looking at the fine animals.

At noon Joey met his parents at the big eating concession stand. Eating at the fair was always a highlight for Joey, but today his eyes seemed bigger than his stomach. The food looked good. It smelled good. Joey's stomach just didn't want it.

"Eat up, Son," cautioned his dad. "You'll need your strength to carry home any prizes you may win."

"If I win any," said Joey. "Every kid here is expecting to win as much as I am."

"I know," said his dad. "That's part of the American way of life, Son. We all work our hardest to be the best. You've done your best. In an hour, we'll see if that was good enough."

When the doors were opened, Joey ran to the "Most Unusual Pumpkin" area. When he got there, his albino pumpkin was gone. So were a couple of others that he had considered close competion. He wondered why. Then he saw his dad and Mr. Billings. They were motioning for him to come to them.

Joey's dad let Mr. Billings break the good news. "You won, Joey," he said. "Your ghost pumpkin won, and now the photographer wants to get your picture for the newspaper. With that kind of publicity, you should be able to sell all your pumpkins come Halloween."

Joey felt very happy, but a little nauseous. He was afraid he was dreaming. He had dreamed this dream so many times. He wanted to shout, "I won! I won! I won!" But he knew that would not be proper.

Finally Joey got up the courage to go look at his two other entires. He went first to the biggest pumpkin contest. He didn't know how they would judge that—the biggest in size or biggest in weight. He would soon find out.

He edged over to the spot where he had placed his entry. When it wasn't there, he felt sure it had won something—first, second, or third. He would look for Mr. Billings. He would know. In the meantime, Joey went to see if his Mr. Ugly Scary Jack had survived. When he found that it was gone, too, he had to sit down for a minute.

"I've got to think straight," he said. "I'm too excited to know where to look for my dad and mom, but I really need them right now."

"Joey! Come here. You are needed for pictures!" It was his mother's voice. Oh, how glad he was to have her nearby. He mustn't cry, but he was so glad to see her that he felt the tears might come any minute.

Joey didn't ask any questions. He was afraid the answers would not be what he wanted to hear. But he wondered how long he could go not knowing about the jack-o'-lantern contest, which was his favorite of all.

Mr. Billings was grinning his big, broad grin. "You won, Joey," he said. "Never has any kid won all three pumpkin contests, but you did just that. The newspaper photographer is over here waiting to get your picture. Say, you look a little white. Do you feel OK?"

"I feel sick. My stomach is squeamish. I wanted to win so badly, but now I'm afraid I'm just dreaming. I'm afraid that if I get too happy, everything will just go away," Joey answered.

He saw his dad and Uncle Dennis. The newspaper reporter was coming toward him. He was smiling too.

"It must be for real," Joey breathed a big sigh.

Everybody was talking at once. Everybody was slapping him on the back. The photographer took half a dozen pictures. He said he wanted to be sure he got a super picture of this triple win. Then he took Joey aside and asked him many, many questions. When Joey told him he was going to sell his pumpkins for Halloween jack-o'-lanterns, the reporter asked him how many he had.

"Almost a hundred big ones," Joey said. "I have to give a few to my very special friends, but I figure I'll have nearly a hundred to sell."

"Tell me about your albinos," asked the reporter. "I've never seen an albino before."

"Neither had I," Joey began. "But when I was hunting for something different, that's what I found. Did anyone tell you that those seed cost me fifteen cents each?"

Joey told the reporter everything he could about his project. Then he asked a question: "Do you have any children, Sir?"

When the reporter said that he had three children, Joey invited them out to see his pumpkin patch.

"Come out, and I'll give you an albino for them for Halloween. Come out any day after school," Joey suggested.

When the newspaper article was published, many people drove out to the McClintock's to see the ghost pumpkins. Joey sold them for a high price. Regardless of size, he asked five dollars for each one. No one seemed to mind because they wanted their children to enjoy having an unusual treat on Halloween.

Some people bought other pumpkins, but they paid only $2.50 for them. Joey was raking in money every day. Many people had called and asked him to save them a ghost pumpkin. He had cut those from the vine and put them in the garage with names on them. Then he set aside one for Uncle Dennis's kids, one for Mr. Billings, and one for his teacher. He decided that he would ask everyone he gave pumpkins to if they would save the seeds for him.

"Next year I'm going to grow only albinos," he mused. "That's where the money is—and money is the reason a farmer works."

Every night Joey brought his books up to date and counted his money. He was amazed that people drove out to his house every evening to buy pumpkins. There wouldn't be any left to take to town to sell the weekend before Halloween. He had thought that having a pumpkin stand would be fun, but this was better. Everyone got to see his albino patch. When the news reporter came out, he took a picture of his kids with Joey in the pumpkin patch and put that photo in the newspaper. Joey liked the write-ups in the paper because he could send those to his grandmother in California. It was almost like having her there for the fair.

Finally the yearly 4-H Club award meeting arrived. All the parents would be there. Joey was glad that his mother and father would get to see him receive his prizes. They had both given him much encouragement; and he knew that he could not have won without them. He remembered all those trips he and his dad had made out to

Lake Redman for water. Water was the reason he had won. He wished other parents could know how his mom and dad had helped.

Mr. Billings was in charge of the meeting, but a man from the chamber of commerce awarded the ribbons and the checks. There were five livestock winners, two poultry winners, and several vegetable winners from Joey's school. None of them won higher than second place, but they were winners and everyone was proud of them. Several girls won cooking, canning, and sewing prizes.

Joey was last. Since he knew he was the only first place winner, he had thought he would be first, but Mr. Billings said he had saved the best for the last. He asked Joey to come up on the stage, then he told everyone everything that had happened to Joey. He told about the lack of water, the hailstorm, and the gopher. He told the parents how Joey's dad had hauled the water for him and how his mother had encouraged him. But he made one thing clear: Joey had done all the work. He told how he had never even heard of an albino pumpkin until Joey brought him the seed catalog.

Joey received two checks for ten dollars each as his two first prizes. A fifty dollar savings bond was the prize for the biggest pumpkin. He received a twenty-five dollar check as a bonus from the town merchants because he won all the pumpkin prizes. But the nicest prize of all was the set of encyclopedias he won for the paper he wrote about pumpkins. Joey couldn't believe it—a set of encyclopedias in his own room for all his schoolwork! Mr. Billings said it was worth over two hundred dollars! Joey could hardly wait to call his grandmother and tell her about all his "loot."

Uncle Dennis took his picture, and so did the newspaper reporter. Joey was proud, but he was very aware of all the help he had received. When Mr. Billings asked him if he had anything to say, Joey shocked himself by speaking what had been in his heart for so long.

"I want to thank Mr. Billings and my teacher, my mother and dad, my uncle Dennis and my grandmother for seed money. But most of all I want to thank God. You see, he was the only one I could talk to on those long, hot summer days when I was carrying all that water and hoeing my pumpkin patch. This summer I learned that God is a farmer's best friend.''